OBSIDIAN'S PATH

OBSIDIAN'S PATH

The Myth

J.E.O.R

J.E.O.R
Obsidian's Path

Published by Spines
ISBN 979-8-89569-812-9

CONTENTS

DEDICATED TO THOSE CRAZY
ENOUGH TO NURTURE THEIR
IMAGINATION.

THE MYTH

Do you believe in legends? In myths?
What if I told you that they held truths?
Would you think I'm crazy?

CHAPTER 1

THE TRUTH

Once upon a time, there stood a prosperous kingdom. The king and queen were both respected and admired for their courage and devotion. The kingdom had witnessed great triumph under their rule, and it seemed like the blessings would just keep coming. The royals were expecting their second child.

Months after his birth, the royals held a banquet that lasted two weeks. Every single person in their kingdom attended, excited to see the new crown prince.

On the eleventh day, a storm passed by. "The banquet is canceled today. Alert everyone that they should take cover in their homes." The king demands. Immediately, guards rush to carry out the royal's wish.

The day grew darker and the storm more fierce. Rumbles tore through the lands, "It's okay dear. The storm will pass." The queen comforted her almost two-year-old. Seven. Within a couple of hours the storm calmed, and silence followed for the first time that day.

With the silence rose a banging on the castle doors followed by commotion that ran through the castle's halls. The king, wanting to know what was happening, went to investigate. "I'm sorry but we will not be hosting the banquet today." "Mother?" The first born whispered to the queen. "Stay here." She answers before heading to her husband.

Reaching the throne room, there was a woman with brown hair so dark that it appeared black. The woman looked no older than her, "Please." She begged. "Honey, we can't throw her out." He turns to her in protest. "We can host her for a couple of hours." "No more than that." The queen nodded in agreement.

The woman eagerly bows as her queen steps forward, "Please come, you must be hungry." She says, leading the way. She holds her husband's arm, royal guards following behind.

And true to their word, they host the woman. The storm passes, and the woman stands to make her leave.

"Thank you so much for your hospitality, your royal highnesses. I must take my leave." She says bowing. "You're welcome." The queen responds, making her way to the woman. The royal guards that stand by the room's entrance step behind the woman, ready to protect their queen. "Your highness," the woman says, finally standing upright, "I come with a gift."

"A gift?" The king asks, the woman turns to direct herself at him. "Yes your highness, this was a banquet after all." "Okay, and what is the gift?" The queen asks. "I am a seer. Your second born has been chosen to break generational cycles." "What do you mean, break generational cycles!" The king's voice booms over everything, seemingly mirroring the storm that has just passed.

"Your highness," she starts, eyes glued to the queen, "shadows follow your family. They always have. Your son has been chosen to either beat them or die trying." "Get her out! Now!" The king demands to the guards, who drag the woman away. She says nothing.

CHAPTER 2

THE DISFORTUNE

Time passed, and as the young royals grew, the queen kept her eyes on them. Attention divided heavily on her first and third. The first because she needed to make sure that the heir to the throne was as stable as the sun itself. Her third because he resembled water, wielding both beauty and chaos if he so wished it. Her attention was unneeded, in her eyes, for her second son. She did not neglect him, she gave him love and attention but her second son became much like the moon, independent and distant, cold.

Regardless, her second son grew up with her other two sons: all stubborn, all strong-willed, all powerful in their own right. But what no one could see was that the second son was constantly being followed. His shadow holding intangible strength. Everywhere he went, the shadows followed, an unwavering opponent.

And before long, the royals had a new addition to their bloodline: a daughter. The royal princess became the earth, the land. She became both the opposite and the same as the third-born. Together, the energies of the four royals mixed well.

When the second royal turned 15, Moon began to cover more

and more of his skin. The more people saw, the more he tried to hide.

"Moon, What is that?" The queen asked. "What is what?" The queen grabbed his wrist and lifted the sleeve of his robe to see his skin. "How did you get this?" She asked, concern evident in her voice, "It's nothing." Moon pulled his hand away and covered it again, bruises and black lines collaging his skin.

The young prince never gave his mother an answer. She had no clue what was happening; she never saw him get hit, and what could make the black lines? The queen demanded that the guards find the woman who had been at the eleventh banquet.

Knowing that she would not get an answer from her son, the only option she had was to wait for the woman to be found. Then, on the eleventh full moon of that year, the crowned royals were awakened by their guards.

They rushed to the throne room, and there she stood, the woman from all those years ago. Life had been good to her; she looked exactly as she did back then. "Your highness." She bowed. "Hi, please stand. I..." the woman lifted her hand to silence the queen. Sensing the uproar, the queen gestured for the guards to remain put.

"Your highness, it is time for your second to start his journey." "What does that mean?" The king interjects, "Please." The queen adds, desperation in her voice. "You must send him away." Before anything else can be said, she throws some powder above herself. Seeing this, everyone darts away. As the powder settles on her, everyone just stares, understanding what she had just done. They would never get any more answers from her.

CHAPTER 3

ESCAPE

"They're going to send me away." The second born thought to himself, rushing up to his room, tears pricking his eyes. Without waiting for anything else the prince packed a bag leaving behind the room that was once his.

On his way through the corridors, he froze at the sound of her voice, "Brother?" "Shhshhshh." He whispered to her, "Go back to bed." "Where are you going?" She asks, rubbing her eyes. "I...I have to go." She hugged her older brother as she began to cry, "I don't want you to go," she whispered into his shoulder.

"I will always be with you. I will speak to you every night." "How?" She asks. He answers, pointing to the window that frames the moon at the end of the corridor, "I am Moon after all." She chuckles through her tears before lightly slapping his arm. "You're not really the moon."

"Oww..." he grabs where she hit him, "You're so strong." "No I'm not." To prove his point, he starts acting as though he has no control of his arm. Lifting it and letting it fall down, "look what you've done." "Stop." She laughs and jokingly pushes him. Before her smile is replaced with a fresh set of tears. "I don't want you to go." He holds her face in his hands caressing her cheeks, "I know. But I have to. I promise I will see you someday." He then holds up his pinky finger and she gives him hers.

He carries her to bed, gives her a goodnight kiss, and vanishes into the night.

Outside the castle he approaches a secret friend, a guard, "Help me." He whispers. The guard whips around pointing his sword at the intruder. "My prince." He lowers his weapon, "You should not be out here. Please allow me to escort you to your chamber." He extends his hand, gesturing the direction in which the prince should walk.

"I need your help." "Young royal?" "You will escort me outside of the kingdom." "Moon I can get beheaded." the guard whispers angrily as he holds onto the prince's arm and starts pushing him to the direction he had suggested earlier. "Let go." The prince demanded.

"Young royal..." "Your loyalty is to the crown. You will escort me outside of the kingdom." "Moon..." "I will leave with or without your help." The prince says, instantly heading toward the side gates.

The guard, his friend since childhood, gets on his knee, "My prince, I Harold, swear my loyalty and my life to serve you." The prince looks at him. This is real. The oath of commitment.

"Stand. We must go." The prince once again turns to the gate, "Your majesty, follow me." The prince turns, but his guard is already leaving. The guard leads the prince down through a part of the castle he had never been through. Before entering, Harold grabs a large, worn robe. "Put this on." The prince puts it on, and the guard makes sure that he is fully covered.

"Here." He tries to hand the prince some dirty shoes, but instead of grabbing them the prince just looks at them in disgust. "Yea, I will not wear that."

"Your majesty." "NO." They stare at each other in silence before the guard backs down. "Follow me, quietly."

The guard starts leading the way, knowing exactly where to

go. Knowing the movements of the guards, he knows that there is a small window for their exit out of the royal grounds.

The coast is clear; the guard leads the way, opening the gate, "Your majesty, come on." He whispers looking around. "Is that a dungeon?" "No it's not." Steps echo through the halls. They're running out of time. Without any warning, the guard tugs the prince into the gate, throwing him down to close the gate softly.

"Oww." Harold darts to cover the prince's mouth. It's funny, if they were found now, it would look like the guard was kidnapping the royal prince. The guard is basically dragging the prince with him, his hand still covering his mouth.

He pushes through some foliage leading them into the center of a stream. Finally the guard lets the prince go. "How dare you?" The prince pushes off of him. "I got you out didn't I?" He says stepping into the stream. "Don't walk away."

Feeling the dark behind him, the prince decides to step into the light as he rushes to catch up to his guard.

CHAPTER 4

SEVEN YEARS LATER

The prince had left his old life and built a new one from the scraps of what remained. His kingdom was now a quarter of the size of his parents' kingdom. It had been a long journey, and with the help of his cabinet, he was succeeding. But at night, the shadows crept. The darkness that the prince once fought in his dreams now filled his life.

The darkness had expanded to his land; worry ran through his kingdom. The prince stood at the highest tower of his castle, looking out to the west fields. What once grew in abundance was now prone to wither.

"Your majesty." "Yes Allura?" She steps closer, "Your majesty, you have people who demand to see you." "They can't demand anything. Do they know who they're talking to?"

"Paige," the Prince, now King, turns around, "It's okay. They have a right to worry." "Whatever." She responds heading out of the tower. The king looks at Allura, "Shall we?"

The king sits on his throne, forming a V with his cabinet. In front of the king stand Allura and Paige, and in front of them stand Harold and Sebastian. The king gestures to the guards for the doors to be opened.

As soon as the doors open, the people flood the throne room. "What are we going to do?" "What is going on?" "What are you going to do?" "It's your fault!" "What is happening to our crops?" "What is happening to the land?" Chaos fills the throne room as voices erupt from every crevice of the room.

The king stands, silencing the chorus that rang through the walls, "I understand that you are all worried and scared about the darkness that has taken over the land. However, I assure you that we are looking not only for the solution but for the reason for its growth. Please go back home and report any changes to the palace. Thank you." With that, the king left, followed by the rest of his cabinet. His subjects exited, some content knowing that answers were being sought and others complaining about the quick dismissal.

"Your highness, what are we going to do?" The king stops at the doors to his room, "I don't know." He answers before disappearing behind them.

Restlessness filled the king's kingdom. The king's subjects received no answers, and almost the whole kingdom had been consumed by the black.

But the castle remained untouched by the darkness. The castle sparkled in comparison to its surroundings. A speck of light in the middle of all-encompassing darkness.

Then one fateful night, when the king could not sleep, he climbed to the highest tower of his castle. The room was filled with crystals of all sizes, and walls covered in mirrors; the room glowed with the radiant moonlight. His lands were covered in a blanket of black.

But as he scanned the land his eyes got stuck on something, a pop of color. He looked through the telescope that was set up to his left in search of the speck of color. A rose. A rose, strong and red, stood tall in the middle of the black void.

The king rushed to the rose, and as his fingers wrapped around the stem, the darkness diminished. Seeing the power held within the rose, he picked it, took it straight to his bedroom, placed it in a tiny flask on his desk, and went to bed.

Calm replaced what was once chaos.

CHAPTER 5

ELUSIVE DARK

The king was awoken by cheers. Cheers so loud that they seemed to shake the ground itself. Opening his doors he was greeted by Sebastian, "Your majesty." He said bowing, "what is going on Sebastian?" "It is the land," the king rushes past, heading to the front, "what about the land?" "It's clear, your highness. The darkness is gone." Stepping out to the front balcony he saw the vibrancy that had seeped back into the veins of his kingdom.

Darkness was only where it belonged: in the shadows.

Everything was fine for a couple of months.

Day after day, color laid upon the land, smiles on the faces of his subjects. But the smile of the king grew heavy. The battles he once had to fight inside himself had returned. Exhaustion consumed the king.

Night after night, the darkness would come back and begin to creep into the palace, something it had never done before. Confusion and worry filled the staff of the palace; no one knew where the darkness came from.

What no one could see was that the king was constantly fighting against the darkness, but no matter what he did, the darkness continued to seep deeper into the confines of his castle.

No one had any clue how the darkness worked or what it was after. “It’s after me.” The king would whisper to himself every night in preparation for the fight against the darkness he would have in his sleep.

After a couple of weeks the darkness had been cleared. A knock rattled the king’s doors to his room, “The darkness has vanished from the castle. We are free from the darkness.” Harold cheered behind the closed doors. The king turns to lay on his side, giving his back to the door. “Your Majesty?” “I’m fine Harold. I just need some rest.” “Okay your highness, i'll be sure to inform everyone to not disturb your sleep.” With that Harold was gone and the king laid still in a cloud of darkness.

His room consumed in black.

CHAPTER 6

EVERGREEN

To everyone else the darkness was a talk of the past. A confusing chapter that had thankfully ended, the darkness was gone. But that darkness was now the only thing surrounding the king. The king had become a prisoner of his own room.

Standing in front of his desk, the one that held a mirror above it, the one that still held the lively rose in a flask made of diamond and gold, only the flask was now painted black. Looking at his eyes in the mirror, he could only say four words, "Maybe I chose wrong?" The king whispered.

That night, the king had the best sleep of his life. There was no fight; there was just sleep. The king awoke well rested and calm.

But that calm was broken by screams and chaos. His eyes flew open, and he darted up, shock taking over.

His room was devoid of the darkness. Had the good night's sleep taken away the darkness? He stepped out onto his balcony, darkness covering everything.

He darted out of his room only to see that it was spreading, covering everything in its coat of black. The only thing that kept its color was his room.

The king ran back to his room, the rose being the only thing on his mind. Tearing through the doors, he saw it: a now dead rose in a flask of diamond and gold. "Maybe I chose wrong." He repeated, remembering the phrase he had used last night. The king turned his head to his right, looking out of the open doors to his balcony.

He began to pack; he would go to the darkest part of his kingdom, searching for answers. Answers he would hopefully find in a cave that lay on the tallest mountain.

The king snuck out of his castle and into the horse stables. As luck would have it, one of the horses was ready to be mounted, Sebastian's.

"Your majesty, who would have thought we would meet like this again." The king turned to see Harold. "Moon are you running away from your kingdom again?" "Harold. I am still your king." "Of course. Do you need my help to run away again?" He asks.

"Harold, mind your place." Harold bows, showing that his loyalty still lies with his majesty. "I am not running away; I want to find an answer." "Then let us help." The king turns to the voice. "Paige, how long have you been there?" "Ehhh, long enough." She shrugs.

"Your majesty, we have sworn to keep you safe. Where you go we shall follow." "Sebastian. No." "You should not go alone." "Allura." "Your majesty, you should not go alone." She repeats, giving the king a stern look. Of course she's right, of course they're right. The king knew that he may encounter dangers on the path. But how could he ask them to give their lives for answers that may not exist.

Taking a deep breath, the king turns to face Harold, "Harold, Allura, both of you will stay. I trust you to keep my kingdom safe." He then turns to look at Sebastian and Paige, "Sebastian, Paige, you're with me." "Hell yea." Paige jumps off the beam where she is seated.

"Do you need some time to get ready?" The king asks his two

friends who will be joining him. "Nope." They both answer, Sebastian getting their ride ready, "Really?" The king asks in disbelief. "Yea. I always have my bag of emergencies ready to go." Paige answers. Sebastian follows, "And I knew you would want to go looking." "How?" "It was just a matter of when."

"Let us get your carriage ready." "No." Sebastian answers before the king does, finishing setting up a second horse. "It will attract too much attention, we will take horses." "Paige can't ride." The king cuts in, watching as Sebastian mounts his horse, "She will ride with me." Paige heads to Sebastian and with his help settles onto the horse. "Shall we."

Carefully, Sebastian leads the way out through a hidden passage. "Seb, how do you know about this passage?" "Well being one of the workers in charge of building your palace comes with its perks." "Does that mean that there are more hidden passages?" Paige asks, making note of where the entrance was and through which arches to cross to reach the exit.

"Yes. A group of us built secret passages in case of an emergency." "Why wasn't I told where the passages are?" The king asks, speeding up so that he can be right next to Sebastian's black horse. "We decided it would be better if we kept the information to ourselves until the emergency demanded its existence to be known."

"Does that mean that you broke your agreement?" Seb looks at the king, confusion on his face, "You know, because I doubt this classifies as an emergency." "You're right. This isn't really an emergency, but we needed it to leave unseen." He pulls his horse ahead again. Maybe I shouldn't have said anything, he thinks to himself as he follows behind the black horse.

CHAPTER 7

TRUST

Five days had passed, and the trio had to flee for their lives. In the moonlight, the king looked down at his reflection in the water, trying to distract himself from what they had just gone through.

Then the moon's light shimmered; something was down there. The king leaned closer, trying to get a better look.

Without any warning, something jumped out of the water, just barely missing the king. The canoe rocked back and forth as the water grew restless, and the three rushed to grab their weapons. Sensing something, the king ducked, turning to face the sky as his sword sliced above him.

He saw as a torso flew by, skin catching on the sword, painting it red. Screeching could be heard before the canoe was tipped over. In the water, the three struggled, red seeping out of their bodies as claws kissed their skin.

Whatever they were, they moved fast. Moon sees Paige tinker on her arm device and seconds later the things are gone. The three crawl onto the river bed, "Ah. Your majesty." "I'm fine Seb." He answers carrying some of their bags further inland. "What were those things?" The king asks Paige who is laying on her back. “The River Lee.” “I thought those things were myths, legends.” “Well there are some legends that are true.” She answers sitting up.

“What did you do to them?” She lifts her left arm to show off her baby, “I used some vibrations that are fatal to them if they are exposed for long enough.” “We should keep moving.” “Can’t we rest a bit?” She asks, but he answers by walking away.

With their canoe gone, they chose to move by foot through the woods. There are very few places to hide since the woods have begun to die. The green long gone, leaving only shades of brown and gray.

“Sebastian, we should get some rest.” He turns ready to argue with the king, “Seb, he’s right we need to rest.” Defeated, Seb agrees, “Very well, we’ll make camp here.” He looks around, it’s a small clearing but it offers the most protection with three big boulders.

The king goes to the middle digging a small hole and putting some dry leaves inside. “I’m going to get some wood.” He stands walking away. “Your majesty!” Sebastian begins to walk after him but Paige puts her hand against his chest, “I’ll go. You stay.” “Don’t go too far.” “Sure thing father.”

“Moon," she calls before reaching his side, “are you okay?” “Why wouldn’t I be?” She hits him playfully on his right bicep with the back of her hand. He grabs his bicep and looks at her, gasping, “How dare you?!” He says jokingly. She shrugs.

A smile creeps onto both their faces. “You know I could have you executed for that.” “Oh come on, for a little pat? After all we’ve gone through?” She asks giving him puppy eyes. They both laugh. “I didn’t say I was going to; I just said I could.” “But you won’t because you love me.” “Don’t push it.” He says plucking up some big branches.

“Why did our cuts stop bleeding?” Paige gets some branches from around, “When a mermaid cuts someone, they’ll only bleed underwater.” “Why?” “Ummm I don’t know.” “You’re the

'Smartest Person Alive' how do you not know?" He says starting to head back to their campsite.

"Ohhh I'm sorry your royal ass. I'll be sure to ask them next time they're trying to kill me." She responds rushing to his side and bumping into him, a chuckle flowing out of both of them.

CHAPTER 8
JOIN ME

The fire burns. They sit around the fire, eating some of the food they got from the town they passed through. Sebastian stands, leaning against the top rock, ready to jump into action should he have to. Paige is seated to the far left of the king, who is sitting directly in front of Sebastian.

Silence surrounded the trio, and in that silence, the pain that filled the king thrived. How many of his subjects wanted him dead? How many were truly by his side? For how long? Why?

"Your majesty?" Sebastian breaks the silence, sensing something is wrong. "Did you know?" The air grows as cold as ice; in an attempt to lighten the mood, Paige cuts in, "How long do you think it will take to get there?" "No." Sebastian answers the king.

"You must have known. You had us buy clothes so worn that they would serve better as rags. You had us be covered in dirt to appear as disheveled as the clothes we wore, so don't lie to me. Did you know?" "I don't think this is the right time to...okay" Paige stops herself after seeing the king give her a warning look. The king stands.

"Did you know?" He asks, stepping closer to the man who stands before him, a full foot taller. "Yes." He answers. "How long has this been happening?" Sadness can be seen on the king's face, slightly obscured by anger. “Your majesty.” “Sebastian, answer me.”

“Eleven months.” “That’s why the guarding posts were increased.” Seb nods in response. “AHHH!” The king screams, crumbling onto the ground before rushing to get his sword. Paige gets on her pulsing wave to see who is around while Sebastian tries to make out figures, staying behind the boulder he was leaning on for cover.

It’s hard to see anything with the light of their fire. Silence. There is nothing.

Then the sound of sticks breaking followed by screams. The noise only lasts half a minute before the silence returns into the night.

The king feels a familiar creep of darkness. He turns and swings his sword to harm the dark, but he is stopped. The king is frozen, with the blade of his sword drawing a little bit of blood from someone's neck. “Sebastian!” Paige shouts, pointing at the king. Rushing to protect his king, Sebastian jumps over the boulder. “Enough.”

He says, freezing Sebastian and Paige where they are. “Who are you?” Paige asks. The guy is slightly taller than the king, with jet black hair. “Why do you have a mullet?” The king asks. “It’s not a mullet! It’s a wolf cut.” “Are you a lone wolf, or can we expect others? Ahh.” “Stop, don’t hurt him!” The guy looks up at Sebastian, who is frozen in midair. "Don’t hurt him? He hurt me!” “We’re sorry. Moon apologize.” “What?! He snuck up on me. Why should I apologize?” “And why should I?" The guy asks, exchanging a death glare with the king. “He is the king.” The guy turns to Sebastian, then to Moon. He unfreezes everyone and gets on one knee, head bowed. Sebastian lands on the floor behind them. “My apologies your majesty. My name is Night.”

“Night.” The king repeats, “Stand.” Following the command, he stands. “My apologies I did not mean to cause you and your...” he looks around, seeing the two others, “Your party, any harm.”

Paige rushes to tend to the cut adorning the king’s back, “If you didn't want to harm us, why did you aim at the king?" She asks as she works on bandaging the king. "Stand away." Sebastian warns, sword directly at the side of Night's throat.

Night does not listen, eyes locked on the king's. "Step back." The king says and Night once again follows. "Your majesty, I bow to you on my name that I am not at fault for your injury." "If it wasn't you then who?" "Scavengers." The king breaks their eye contact for the first time noticing how Sebastian tenses at the mention of who attacked. They had been followed from the town. "Sebastian, remove your weapon." He hesitates in doing so.

"Join us." The king says, going to sit around the fire. "Of course my king." He sits to the king's right, with Paige and Sebastian following. The night transfers them to sleep, one thing on the king's mind.

What did I do wrong?

CHAPTER 9

BACK

Dawn came but last night's pain did not vanish with the night. The king made his way back to the river. Sitting by its edge a calmness flowed through the king with the morning breeze, "Your majesty." The king turned to see Night standing there, "You have some really long nails." He says looking at his fingers, Night chuckles, "May I join you?" The king nods. Night sits beside him, "Why did you come alone?" He asks, eyes locked onto the flowing water, mirroring the king.

"I had to..." he looked down at his hands, "clear my mind." After a small pause, Night answers, "I can't cut my nails." to the first thing his king said, leaving the sore topic out of focus. "What do you mean you can't cut them?" He asks, holding the hand that Night has offered him. "I tried when I was younger. Everyone would stay away from me because of them." The king moved his attention to Night's face, "People would call me 'The son of Grim'." Night tore his eyes from the king's, looking back to the water.

"Do you believe that?" The king asks, shocking Night. Night looks back at the king with a small smile on his lips before it disappears again as he turns away. "I used to. But after living alone in these mountains, I learned that I am not what they wanted me to be." "And what is that?" "A monster."

The king smiles, caressing the long nails. "Do you think that's how people view you?" "Yes." Night answers coldly, "Everyone I've ever met thinks that of me, except for me. I don't think I'm a monster" "And me." Night whips his head to face the king, "You really mean that?" He whispers, almost afraid of hearing his king change his mind. "Yes." Night begins to move closer to the king, slowly closing the gap between them.

"Here." The king says, removing one bangle from each hand. "What?" Night looks at the golden bangles that lay in his palms, "Why?" "You are no monster, and I am offering you a place in my cabinet." His eyes widen, "But that is a sacred position. I couldn't take up such a special place."

The king gets closer, "Why not? I thought you said you believed you aren't a monster." "I do believe that." "Then trust me." Moon helps put the bangles around Night's wrists, they are so close, "Always."

"Moon!" Paige yells. They pull away just in time as Sebastian and Paige come into view. "There you guys are." "Why is he looking at me like that?" Night asks, pointing at Sebastian, jewelry dangling from his wrists. "Oh he just thought that you had captured the king."

"Sebastian, I'm fine. Can you please ease up." "You're majesty it is my duty to protect you." "As is mine." Night cuts him off, anger filling his face, pulling the king closer to him. The king blushes, "Okay both of you that is enough. I can't have you both fighting." The king stands dusting himself off before offering his hand to Night, who eagerly takes it. "Paige" Sebastian whispers. "I know. It's too late."

"So shall we?" The king asks, "We're not going in there again right?" He points to the river. "No your majesty. We will head up through the woods. Follow me." He begins to walk, followed closely by the king. Paige stays behind, creating distance from Seb and Moon.

"Night, will you walk with me?" Night stops, waiting for her to catch up, "Sure." The cracking of dry leaves and small twigs fills every step, the crackling being the only thing breaking the silence.

"Night, how are you still human?" He looks at her wide eyes. "You know what I am?" "Of course. I am the smartest person alive." She answers, a smirk on her face, remembering how the king had mocked her for using that very title. Self appointed of course.

"How did you find out?" "Your nails." He looks at his nails. No one knew, how did she find out just by his nails? "Plus. You turned in your sleep." "Oh." " Yea I had to stop Sebastian from killing you as you slept." "Thank you." "Are you after the king?"

"Over here!" The four look back and they see people running directly to them. "Run!" The king pulls away from the group, "This way!" He yells for the three to follow. The king leads them through the trees. He is being led, but where? The king takes a hard right and runs up to some stairs with a door at the top.

He opened the door, "Come on!" He gestured at the three. "Your majesty, are you crazy? The door goes nowhere!" "Your majesty, we have to keep running." Night looked at them, "Do you trust your king?" "Yes." They both answer, "Then move it." He rushed up the stairs, followed closely by Paige and Sebastian behind her.

They go through, the king being the last one to go through, closing the door behind him. "Where the hell did they go?!" The people chasing them grow frustrated over the loss of the king. A crack is heard, "Over here!!" They yell continuing their chase after a king that is no longer on the run.

"What is this place?" Sebastian asks, their attention finally on the room where they have ended up. Everything is made of rock. There are books on a rock shelf, lamps on rock tables, and cushions on a rock couch.

"Who are you?!" Sebastian demands, sword ready to fend for their lives. She just smiles. "How can we trust you?" "That's it.

Sebastian has lost his mind. I knew it was only a matter of time."
"Paige." The king calls her name. Then, in their minds, they hear her, "He hasn't lost his mind."

CHAPTER 10

REVELATION

"Your majesty, it is nice to see you again." She gestures for them to sit. "So what are you?" Paige asks, sitting on the armrest, sliding to lay on the couch, her feet dangling over the armrest.

"I don't remember ever meeting you." The king says, taking a seat on the couch. Night joins him, sitting next to the king on the armrest.

"Of course you don't." She turns to Sebastian, "Please, sit." Hesitantly, he sits, sword standing on the floor next to the seat he's on. "When I met you," She says, going for a teapot that's close by, "You were a prince. Not even a year old." She shares a smile with the king before pouring the tea into four cups.

"We are grateful for your hospitality, but we will not be drinking that." Ignoring what she has been told, she continues to finish pouring the four cups. "You need it for the end of your journey." She clarifies, taking the last available seat, furthest from Sebastian.

"Who said we are on a journey?" "Young child one does not come across my home unless one is traveling." "We are still not drinking that." She glances at Sebastian before settling on the king.

"Your majesty, the darkness has decreased, has it not." "No. My land..." "I do not speak of the land." She cuts him off. "Your majesty, I'm talking about the darkness that has followed you from a very young age. I'm talking about the darkness that has harmed your body, soul, and mind."

"What is she talking about?" "They don't know? The people closest to you, don't know." The king picks up the tea cup closest to him. Seeing that, Sebastian grabs his sword and scoots to the edge of his seat, "Your majesty." He does not tear his eyes away from the cup in his hands. " Put the cup down."

"How could I ever tell them when I myself don't understand what it is." Using the armrests she helps herself up. "You are inbound." Paige's face grows serious and she adjusts herself to be seated the way the rest are. Judging by Paige's reaction this is serious, worry fills Sebastian, "Your majesty. Put the cup down." He repeats. "What does that mean?" Night asks the lady.

"Every person who has ever lived has had to fight against internal demons. But few are Inbound." She says picking up a picture from her fireplace. "Inbound people are ringers of death." She dusts the picture before placing it back down. "Death itself will seek those inbound. None live past eleven years old." "But he's twenty three." Paige stops her.

"Yes. You are the second." "Second?" She continues, "People who are inbound are filled with imbalance. They do not change, and so death can reach them. But you." She pauses, "You are constantly changing. Your internal imbalance is always changing. Always searching for balance." "But how does that have anything to do with the darkness that has fallen upon my land?"

"You're close." Not expecting her to take such a long pause, they exchange looks, trying to understand. "The closer you get, the darker your world will seem." She goes to stand before the king, "Peace, growing darkness, disappearance of darkness, the darkness returns worse, devoid of light, and then it's gone."

They look at her, confused. "That is the order in which your journey must go. In order to live, you must accept it as your own. Acceptance of the darkness is your last step."

"That's it?" Everyone turns to look at Sebastian. "Hasn't anyone ever told you? Acceptance is one of the hardest things to do." She places her hands on the kings.

"I've seen you live to an old age. This will not be the only battle you will face, but it is one of the most important." Slowly, she lifts the cup towards his lips, "Fully embodying who you are, who you can be, and who you are meant to be."

"Your majesty." Sebastian stands ready to kill the old hag if harm befalls the king. Slowly, the cup meets his lips, and the king drinks all of the red liquid. Night grabs the cup that was in front of the king's. Sebastian reaches to stop him, but it's too late. Night has drunk it.

The lady grabs the teapot and takes it back to where it goes. "Your majesty," Paige holds his arm, "how do you feel?" "You two have to drink yours." Paige and Sebastian share a look before she reaches for her cup. "Paige!" Sebastian stops her. "Sebastian, we don't know what it will do." "Exactly!" "Two of us have already taken it." "And that makes it better?" He asks, eyes widening. "You have to drink yours." The lady says to him, sitting in her seat.

"Fine." Angry, he walks to grab the last cup and downs it. As soon as he drinks it, everyone starts feeling its effects. "What did you do?" Sebastian slurs the words together, stumbling back to his seat. Dizzy, he turns to his right and sees the three with their eyes closed, and seconds later, he joins them. "Now is the time."

The king awoke in the midst of darkness, the small amount of light coming from the bangles on his wrists. "You guys?" He whispers. "My king." "Night" at least he's not alone. "Night where are you?" "I don't know. I think we should wait." "No, we have to get out."

"Your majesty, I can't protect you separated like this." "You won't have to." "But." "Do you trust me?" The king asks abruptly.

After some silence, Night responds, "Yes." "Then we will move forward." "Okay. But please, be careful."

The king smiles looking to the wall to his left, where Night's voice is coming from, "I promise." He says touching the wall before beginning to walk through.

It was a maze filled with echoes and hallucinations.

What once plagued the king's mind was now surrounding him.

CHAPTER II

TORCH

The deeper the king went, the more that the darkness attached to his skin, painting it black. "Your majesty?" Worry filled the cave walls. The king was tired, stumbling through, struggling to stay upright.

He leaned on the walls, using them as support, "Yes?" "Please stop moving. I can't lose you." Night's voice cracked just at the thought of his loss.

The king stopped moving, resting to catch his breath, his back against the dark wall. "I have to keep going Night. I have people who rely on me." "Your majesty, you have people who prefer your safety." "I do not want my safety to come from cowardice. I have to find my answers." "Moon." "You will never lose me." Moon assures before he begins his walk again.

Light. Red light shines through the gaps in some vines, "Do you see that?" "The red light with a crown symbol?" "What?" The king asks, getting closer to the vines.

He looks around, investigating, when he finds a symbol of a claw. "Mine has a claw symbol... It reminds me of your nails." He smiles through the pain.

Looking through one of the gaps, he sees a plant as beautiful as a flower. "Night!" He shouts as some vines open and let him through. "Moon!"

Night rushes over, "You look rough." He whispers, holding onto one of the vines. "How did you get through?" "I don't know, the bangles started shining and opened the way."

"Why aren't my bangles doing that? They came from the same set." He says frustratingly. "I...don't know." "Do you feel that?" The king asks, reaching his hand towards the plant. Night moves out of the way and faces the plant, "Warmth." "Yea."

Night moves from the vines, "Night what are you doing?" "Getting the plant for you." He says, briefly pausing to look at the king before continuing his path to some stairs. Rumbling roars through the cave, "Get out of my head!" The king yells at the shadows that have plagued his life, pain shooting through his body.

The king falls to the ground, eyes squeezed shut, willing the pain away. Opening his eyes, the king sees feet. The king moves his eyes upward only to find that the shadow has his face. "What are you?" The king asks, rising. The shadow laughs, "I am you." The shadow walks around, and from behind, he whispers into the king's ear, "Your fears." He moves to the other ear, "Your shame."

The king turns to meet the shadow's eyes, "That can't be. Ever since I left my parent's kingdom I have been fighting and mending all of my..." the king freezes, realizing what was causing the darkness, "My shadows." "You're right, your highness but there is still something holding you captive in this life." "Ahhh." Night screams.

The king turns to run toward Night but is stopped by the shadow holding his wrist, burning where skin meets shadow. The king looks at the shadow, determination on his face. Amused, the shadow smiles, "Are you really ready to remove the rest of your chains?" Night can be heard tumbling down the stairs, the searing pain tingling his skin. "Night!" The king yells, looking at the vines.

The king steps closer to the shadow, "I am done hiding who I am." "We'll see about that." With that, the shadow merges directly into the king.

Taking a couple of deep breaths, the king steps toward the vines, "I think I can squeeze through." He tells Night. The king crawls through a very tight gap in the bottom right corner of the passage.

The king crawled forward, ignoring the roaring cries of his skin as it got caught on the teeth of the surrounding vines. Finally through, the king rushed to Night's side, ignoring the fresh blood running down his torso.

"Night. Are you okay?" "Ahh. Moon you're hurt." "It's just a little blood... Don't give me that look." Night smiles, rolling his eyes, "Stubborn as ever." "Oh quiet, you know you like it." "Yes, I do." The silence is strong, "Umm." The king clears his throat, "I think that's the answer. I have to get it."

"Your majesty." "I'll be quick." The king pushes away and approaches the stairs. He begins the climb, but to his surprise, he feels nothing; there is no pain. Reaching the top, stone heads begin to pop out from the walls and ceiling. "Moon!" Night rushes over, the heads charging for their attack as the head's mouths fall open one by one.

The one directly in front of the king is the first to trigger, fire flowing from its mouth. Night jumps in front of him just in time, back catching fire. "The plant!" He yells, the king kneels down and Night follows above him. Fire flashes before everything goes dark. A black dome covering them as the heat slowly creeps in. The king digs like his life depends on it and he rips it out of the ground.

In an instant, the heat is no longer rising, and the dome disappears. "Your majesty!" Sebastian and Paige run over. "I'm okay." "You're burning up." The lady fills a bowl with room temperature water and rags. "Here." She offers it to Paige. "How are we back here?" The king asks.

Sebastian is moving Night's hair out of his face. "Here." Paige places the bowl between them, tending to Moon while Sebastian tends to Night as they ignore the king.

"Goodbye. It was an honor to see who you've become, your majesty." The lady vows, and their surroundings are no longer rock but carpet.

"Your majesty!" Harold rushes over, "I'm fine." The king says sitting up, "I'm fine." He repeats directly at Paige to convince her. "Night!" He looks at Night then to Harold, "Get me the royal healer." "Yes your majesty." He answers before darting out of the room.

Over the following days, the darkness began to be absorbed into the king, but this time it was accompanied by peace. Looking to his royal garden, calm filled the king, "I chose wrong." He said to himself, a smile on the king's face as he saw the healthy plants that now adorned his castle. "Beautiful." "Yes they are." The king responded, turning to meet Night's eyes.

The End

ONE THOUSAND YEARS LATER

"And they were roommates"

AUTHOR'S NOTE

Welcome to my universe
-WMTE-

BONUS

OBSIDIAN'S PATH

THE MAN

CHAPTER

"Mom." I whine, "Why can't I play outside?" She runs her hands through my hair as I lean all my weight against her side, "Because I said so." "But that's not fair." I detach myself from her, and stomp out of her room. "Obsidian!" She yells after me, but I don't want to see her.

Why is she so mean to me? I think to myself walking through the palace halls. "Carnelian and Marine can play outside."

The castle is so big that through my exploration nothing around me is familiar anymore. I'm lost, I think to myself when from the corner of my eyes I see something move. "Hey!" I shout as I begin to chase after the movement.

I turn the corner only to find that there is no one. "Hello?" I say walking down a corridor with no movement. "Hello?" I call out, opening the double doors at the end of the corridor, "WOW."

Towering green is everywhere I look, the room looks like a forest. The size of this room alone is impressive, a greenhouse five stories tall. I walk off the path onto the green on the floor. Reaching down I gasp when I touch the weird green thing. It's not as soft as it looks.

I lay, making sure the flower I carefully tuck behind my ear does not fall. I lay, watching as the yellow turns into a golden orange hue that paints the room.

The calm is broken by the growling of my stomach. "Time for food." I say, getting up. After dusting myself off I head to the doors, but with every step I take the smell grows.

"What is that smell?" I ask, opening the doors, mouth watering. I breathe in the delicious smell trying to follow its scent. My nose takes lead as it guides me running through the castle corridors.

"Your majesty." the cooking staff say, startled as I burst into the kitchen. They bow as I pass following the smell deeper into the kitchens. There are many places in the palace that I still do not know, the kitchens being one of them.

I keep walking through door after door. "Found you." I say opening one of the doors.

"Oh." I'm met with a small child who has powdered sugar all over his face. "What are you doing?" he darts towards me, pulling me in, and closing the door behind me.

"SHHH. you're going to get me in trouble." He whispers. "Who is going to get you in trouble?" I ask, leaning in, also whispering.

"My mom," he says getting up and walking over to the basket he was indulging in, "I'm not supposed to be here." he continues, handing me a jelly filled powdered donut.

I watch as he grabs a donut from the basket, and bites into it, "Who are you?" I ask. "Oh." He puts the donut on his left hand, wiping his right hand on his clothes before reaching forward. "My name is Harold."

I look at the dirty little boy, his skin a chocolate brown with short curly hair. I grab his hand and shake it, "My family calls me Moon." We let go of our hands, "But I'm not your family," He says, taking a bite of the donut, "do your friends call you Moon too?"

"I don't... I don't have any friends." I confess, looking down to the donut he handed me. He sits, "I'll be your friend." He says, scooting over and taping the spot next to him.

CHAPTER

Night fell over the kingdom, it was 7pm and the royals were seated on their dining table.

"Mom, can we eat?" "No." I answer, calling over one of the guards, "Can you please go and tell Moon that we are waiting for him." The guard nods, bowing before exiting the room.

"Honey, I'm sure he's just tired and is already asleep." "Even if that's the case I would like to know where he is." I turn to Carnelian and Marine, "Did you see your brother on your way here?" "No."

Minutes pass and the four of us are still sitting at the table waiting for Moon. As the time passes, the sound of movement grows.

My husband stands, and opens the doors to the dining room, "What is the meaning of this?" His voice booms over the chaos of guards and staff running from room to room.

"Your majesty," one of the guards stops, bowing, "We were unable to find the royal prince Obsidian." Overhearing the conversation I approach the guard, "What do you mean you can't find Moon." "I'm sorry your majesty." "Stay with the royal children." I command the guard before walking away, my husband following behind me.

He tugs on my hand to catch my attention, "I'll check the servant's quarters." I nod, "I'll check the kitchens." I say before we both go our separate ways.

I burst into the kitchen startling the staff, "Your majesty." I walk past everyone, heading towards the head chef. "Have you seen Obsidian?" She looks at me worried, "Umm yes your majesty. He passed through the kitchen a couple of hours ago but I haven't seen him since."

Turning away I continue through the kitchen checking every door. Asking the same question multiple times, receiving an almost identical answer each time. There is only one door left in the kitchen, and I am almost certain I will not find him here.

Opening the door I am met with the image of two sleeping children: both covered in powdered sugar and jam. "Who is this child?" I ask.

The head chef looks over my shoulder into the walk-in pantry, she gasps. "I'm so sorry, your majesty." "Why are you apologizing?" I ask looking at the sleeping boys, "That's my son. He isn't supposed to be here." She explains looking at the floor as I walk into the pantry.

I kneel down, and lightly shake Moon awake. "Moon." I call softly as he stirs awake. "Come on. You have to take a bath." "Mama I have a friend." he says with a smile on his face as I help him up. "And what is your friend's name?" "Harold." I smile and nod.

Holding Moon's hand we walk out of the pantry. I stop, and turn to the head chef, "You can continue bringing him." She bows before I walk out.

Obsidian and his friend, Harold, became closer as time passed.

My second son grew with my other two sons: all stubborn, all strong willed, all powerful in their own right. And before long our royal bloodline had a new addition, a daughter.

The royal princess became the earth, the land. She became both the opposite and the same as the third born. Together the energies of the four royals mixed well.

CHAPTER

I sit at the dining table. Silence fills the room except for the smug smirk on my father's face, he turns to Marine, "Water, your teachers tell me that you are quite the ladies man." I roll my eyes. "Well of course the girls would go crazy for him, he's so handsome." "He's eleven." I chime in.

"Just because you are incapable of commanding attention does not mean that you have to disrespect your brother." I mockingly chuckle, "I do not have to command attention when it is easily given to me." "If that were true you wouldn't need my help to find a wife."

"I don't need your help." He looks at my mother, "Hon, have you sent a letter to our future daughter-in-law?" "Yes, I am awaiting her response. I also sent her a marriage gift from her betrothed." She smiles at me as if I should be happy with what is going on.

"Why would you do that?!" "Watch it boy." My father calls my attention. "How many times do I have to tell both of you that I do not wish to marry. I do not want her as my bride." "You need someone with experience, so I got you a wife with seven years more experience." "Yea and someone whose heart belongs to another."

My father's smirk drops, not daring to look away from me; daggers in his eyes. "You didn't know?" I ask my mother who is stunned at the new information, "Mother, do you know that Lord Alfer begged father not to chain his daughter to me."

"Shut it!!" My father slams his hand on the table. He stands and leans closer to me, "You are a royal! She is not chained to you, she is honored to have you. You will sit and stop this nonsense." He sits back down, continuing with a lower tone, "You will marry and that is final. Am I clear?" I bow my head, "Yes, your royal highness." I push through gritted teeth.

Tension hangs in the air, especially as my father can't even meet my mother's eyes. "Father," I start, defeated. "What Obsidian?" "Can I at least be allowed to join the ranks?" "We've spoken about this before and my answer remains the same." He answers unwavering.

"My betrothed is a highly ranked warrior, and the greatest shot in the land. I think that I should at least be able to help in her defense." I argue, holding no hope for my father to change his mind.

However, my hopes are answered by my mother, "Of course you should join the ranks." My father looks at her, shocked over her decision to undermine him, "After all he will have to be able to protect his future wife." She says, daring my father to try and oppose her decision.

"Moon, follow me" My mother says standing.

I follow closely behind my mother who takes me to the very top of the castle. Aplace that is restricted to everyone except my mother, and a few staff members.

We walk through the huge doors and walk into an open room with towering walls adorned with all different types of weapons. An older lady, maybe in her sixties, walks towards my mother; gorgeous white hair cascading over her shoulders as she bows. "Your majesty."

"Debra," My mother smiles, "I would like you to train my second son." She looks at me, an eyebrow shooting up, "Hmm." She hums as she makes her way around me. "And in what weapon would you wish for your son to specialize?" "I will leave that up to you but I would like him to specialize in seven."

"Seven?" She asks, "My queen seven is a lot. I would recommend three." "Very well, let's say three, but aim for seven." Debra opens her mouth to say something, but changes her mind. Nodding instead.

"Why are you here?" Debra asks, turning to me. "I am here so that I may be able to protect my betrothed." She shoots a look at my mother.

"And what is the timeframe?" "The eleventh full moon of the upcoming year." She eyes me again before bowing to me, "It will be my pleasure to mentor you, prince Obsidian of the Crystal Kingdom."

CHAPTER

He's slowing down. I think to myself trying to keep my breath steady. We are both tired, fighting to see who loses or who lasts longer. "What are you doing?" I ask, our swords clashing in front of our chests.

We are inches away from each other's faces. "You will not win." He responds, pushing our swords, forcing me to take a step back. I turn around getting out of his way. Losing my push back, he stumbles forward as I grow the distance between us.

"Prince!" I quickly look to my right, and see Tarak sliding a bow and arrow onto the platform. I focus my attention back to my opponent who is charging at me once more. Sword aimed at my chest, the handle close to his chest as he charges left shoulder ahead.

I swing my sword up, sparks flying where our swords make contact. I Lift my sword up, taking his sword with mine. Taking a step forward with my left foot, I bend down to put my left arm in between his legs; using his momentum against him I lift him, and drop him on his back, our swords never breaking contact. Once on the ground I step on the blade of his sword, signaling the end of our fight.

I watch as he sits on his knees, his breath heavy. How dare he attempt to kill me? I ask myself, anger rising. "This outcome seems appropriate." I say, walking to the same stairs I used to get on the platform hours ago. "Why is that?" He hisses out. "Your name is Loss." I answer, walking off in the direction of the castle.

I get into my bathtub full of hot water. I lean back, relaxing into the water, eyes closed, thinking about all the people I met today, and the fact that I won every single fight. Who is Debra?

"Good job today prince." "Debra!" My eyes shoot open as I

scramble to cover myself up. "What have I told you about using my name?" "What are you doing here?"

As if to make us even, she ignores my question, "You did not bow to Loz." "Why would I? He wanted to kill me." The cold crystal of my sword touches my right shoulder. "It is improper not to bow at the end of a one on one; even if they sought your death."

"What if he would've killed me?" "He did not." "But..." she presses the sword to my neck. "No student of mine will act in such a way."

"Okay Deb..." the pressure against my neck increases, "Yes ma'am." I correct, "I will find Loz and apologize for my action." The pressure disappears. She taps my arm with the handle of the sword, "Welcome to group A of the ranks." She says as she walks out of my washroom, sword left on the marble top.

CHAPTER

Swords clash against each other, anger charging every one of my swings. "Moon." "What Harold?" "What's wrong?" He asks, struggling to block my every swing. "Nothing." I swing attack after attack. "This is not nothing." He grunts, frowning at my loss of composure.

Through the anger I begin to forget Debra's lessons; each move, each swing, blood red. In our dance, Harold takes the opening and disrupts my feet.

I tumble, unable to catch my balance, I fall to the ground. "Whatever you're mad at, don't take it out on me." Clapping erupts.

I turn to see the rest of group A watching our match, but my eyes stay on the 'twins'. "Your majesty." Harold bows and offers me his hand. "Harold..." "Ranks!" "Yes sir." We all respond facing our trainer.

"Today is your lucky day. You have your first mission." "Hell yea." Wooos and high fives go through the group that had been watching the fight. Brina just smiles while Jen has her usual smirk. Does that girl do anything other than smirk?

Vazu delegates our objectives, "Brina, Harold, you will be part of the escort team." That means. "Prince Obsidian, Jen, you will have tower duty."

"You have got to be kidding, tower duty?!" So she can do something other than smirk. I think to myself, noticing the distaste that has fallen upon her face. "Everyone has their objectives. Head out."

What a waste of a day, I sigh. This sucks.

I clench my jaw, eyes closing, as I try to keep my breathing stable. "Can you stop!" I snap at Jen who stops hitting the metal railing for the first time in five hours.

"I'm sorry your majesty, is it bothering you?" "Yes." I push through my teeth. "Hmm" she hums before starting up again.

I walk over, grabbing the hand holding the dagger that she keeps banging. "Can you stop?" I repeat. A second dagger making contact with my throat.

"I don't remember giving you permission to touch my stuff." She stares up at me. "I get you're mad we got tower duty, but do you think I'm happy about it?" She does not budge. "Just stop the banging." I demand, letting go of her hand, and walking back to where I was.

I breathe in the cooling wind; taking in the breeze, the silence. In the dark I hear steps approaching. My eyes open just as Jen sits on the railing, "You're weird." "..." "Most men go crazy when they lose to a girl. But you got mad because you didn't lose to a girl." She swings her feet over the rail.

"That isn't the point." "Oh do enlighten me your royal prince." I suck on my teeth, "You wouldn't understand." "No I wouldn't. Unlike you I have had to fight for what I have."

"Sure Jen." I say mockingly, walking away from her to take her old seat.

"How did you do it?" I look down to my hands, "How did you manage to get the prince to be your friend?" "Well, it helped that we met when we were children, but it isn't that difficult; the prince does not take kindly to feeling like a decision has been made for him. So just let him choose." "Crack-a-doodle." Harold looks at me, a small chuckle falling out of his lips.

"What are you laughing at?" I ask, bumping my shoulder with his. "Nothing, it's just always funny to hear you avoid using foul language. Not even the prince is as good as you are." "You're kidding." I grab his arm with both hands, "Can you tell me more about the prince?"

I watch as Harold opens his mouth a couple of times,

changing his mind every time. "The prince likes to feel like he can trust the people who are close to him." "Isn't that a little..." "dumb?" I nod, " He is the prince after all."

"It's a bit more complicated than that. He believes that every one is merely there out of obligation to the king and queen." I sit straight, bring my hands to my thighs. "For the prince it is important to feel like he has earned what he has, because then he can feel like it was his decision, not something that was chosen for him."

"Why the hell are you sulking?" "What does it matter to you?" "Your majesty." "What." I snap my head to face her, her legs still dangle over the railing. "Congratulations on your betrothal." "..." "Why did you choose to wed someone that much older than you? I'm sure you could've found someone around our age."

Turning to look at me, she must have seen something on my face because she instantly changes her tone. "I apologize if I have overstepped." A smile cracks on my lips, "So you can be formal." "Shut up." She turns back around, silence flowing through again.

I walk over to the railing once more. Looking at the view, I take a deep breath, "I had no choice in the matter." "Your majesty." She whispers. My eyes meet hers, I feel a gloss fall over them. If she asks I can just blame it on the wind.

"I am well aware of the way many of the ranks view me. But joining the ranks has been one of the only decisions that has truly been mine." "Your majesty, I'm sorry." "Moon. You may call me Moon."

I begin to walk away, "Be sure to tell Brina she is also allowed to address me as Moon." "Where are you going?" "Their back." I say leaving Jen alone in the tower.

CHAPTER

"The little prince better get here soon." "Did he really say we could call him Moon?" "For the tenth time; Yes, Brina." "I'm sorry I'm just so excited." A huge smile is plastered on her face, "Harold over here." She raises her hand to call him over.

"Twins." He nods. "Ranks!" "Yes sir!" "Grab a bow and arrow, we will be focusing on long range training today." "Harold, where's the prince?" I whisper. "The prince is excused for the day." Vazu responds, eyes on me.

"Moon, What is that?" My mother stops me. "What is what?" She grabs my wrist, and lifts the sleeve of my robe, displaying my skin. Bruises, and black lines collaging my skin. "How did you get this?" She asks, concern evident in her voice.

"It's nothing mother; I'm in a hurry." I pull my hand away, and cover it again. "I have to meet dad." Without another word I rush off to meet my father.

The young prince never gave his mother an answer. She had no clue what was happening. What could make the black lines? The queen demanded for the guards to find the woman who had been at the eleventh banquet many years ago.

Knowing that she would not get an answer from her son the only option she had was to wait for the woman to be found.

"Father," I bow, "why have you asked me to meet you here?" "Do you know what this place is?" He asks, hands resting on the railing as he looks at the water that flows through feeding the only waterfall of the kingdom. The palace was built above a river.

I join him at the railing, "This is where you met mother."

"Yes... You will be meeting your betrothed here." "Father, I don't want this." "Obsidian," he turns to look at me, "you have made that abundantly clear, but you better get it through that thick little head of yours that you will marry, and you better do it quickly. She will be here any moment now."

"What?" "Your highness, the daughter of Lord Alfer is here." He nods to the guard. Turning to me, he grabs my shoulders, "Make me proud." Is the last thing he chooses to say to me before he leaves. Will I ever?

"Your Majesty." I hear a soft voice come from the wall behind me. "My lady." "I do not like that title." "Then what shall I call you?" I ask. Leaning on the railing I look down to my hands, biting the inside of my lips.

"Just, Miss Alfer." "Very well. Miss Alfer." I let the soothing sound of the flowing water calm the thought that neither one of us wants this. Finally, she breaks the silence.

"I brought you a gift." "A gift? I'm sorry I didn't bring a gift for you. But do not worry, I will have your wedding gift before we wed."

Has she changed her mind? "This is not a courting gift, your majesty. It's a birthday gift. You became of age today, did you not?" "Yes." I answer plainly.

The doors to my left open, and a guard steps through, "Your majesty." He bows, opening the box he is carrying, presenting Miss Alfer's gift. "They are beautiful." My fingers lightly caress the bangles.

Two sets of gold bangles covered in diamonds. One set has a lilac diamond at their center, and the second set has a black diamond at their center. "Please take them to my room." "Yes, your highness."

"How did you buy these bangles?" "Are you questioning my morality?" "Of course not, I'm just curious." I step closer to the wall dividing us. "I paid for them with my own money." "Your own money?" I furrow my brows, "What do you do for your money?"

"I'm sure you've heard of my work." I swallow thickly. It can't be, can it? When my father said someone with experience that is not what he meant. Right? "I used money that I had saved from my time as a warrior" "I see, I hope you didn't spend all of it on this gift." "I will admit, it was more than I would've liked." "Sorry."

An awkward silence rolls in. "I. Umm..." "Prince Obsidian." She says, leading the conversation. "Yes?" "I would like to ask for your mercy."

"What do you mean?" "I would like to ask you to reconsider this union." A chuckle falls out of my lips, "That's why the gift was so expensive. Were you trying to buy my compliance?"

"My prince, I'm sure that you could have anyone you would like." "Except for you?" I jokingly blurt out. "I... I have someone who I have sworn myself to." The confession comes as a whisper, as if she has accepted that that commitment is a thing that will no longer happen.

"Tell me about him." I say as I take a seat, back against the wall that divides us.

CHAPTER

Night veils the land in its dominant dark when a banging woke the crowned royals.

"What is it, Vin." I hear my husband growl as I curl into his chest, trying to be carried back to sleep. There is no answer.

I let my eyes open slowly. Carefully, I snake my hand towards the headboard, where I unsheath my dagger.

The room fills with the slow creaking of the doors to our chamber. I pull my hand back mimicking the movement from when I reached forward, dagger now in hand. I feel my husband tense beside me. "What do you want?" I ask, ready to attack.

"Your majesty," is said quickly as light fills the room, "she's here." My husband rises, and I turn to place my dagger in its place, "Who's here?" "The seer, my queen." My head snaps to meet my husband's eyes.

"Are you sure?" I ask as I rush to put my coats on. He answers with a nod. "Take us." My husband demands.

We follow the winding paths in our castle, trying not to make too much noise, but every step we take announces our presence.

Bursting through the double doors to the throne room there she stood, the woman from all those years ago. Life had been good to her; she looked exactly as she did back then. "Your highness." She bowed. "Hi," I approach the seer, "Please stand. I..."

The woman lifts her hand to silence me. Sensing the uproar that will happen for disrespecting me, I gesture for the guards to remain put. A command that they reluctantly follow, ready to defend if they must.

"Your highness. It is time for your second to start his journey." "What does that mean?" "Please." I add in hopes that formality will get us an answer. "You must send him away." "What? WHERE?" My husband interjects once more.

"Your majesty!" Debra shouts, emerging from the side doors of the throne room, "I came as soon as I could." She says to me, as she makes her way to stand behind the woman. Nodding, I turn my attention back to the seer who only smirks, and turns to face Debra.

"So this is where you have hidden." I notice as Debra's hold on her sword handle tightens, before she is holding it up in warning. Seeing Debra's actions, all the guards in the room circle the woman. "Careful witch." She warns. "The fruit of your betrayal has ripened."

"Your majesty!" A royal guard shouts, pulling me away from the seer as she throws some powder above herself. The guard pushes me, wielding his sword he steps in front of me as the other guards watch the powder and the woman from a bigger circle.

I watch from the floor as the powder settles on her. Everyone just stares at her, frozen in high defense. "My love. How dare you throw your queen?!" He shouts, helping me off the ground. His eyes fall on me again, searching for any pain, I lightly shake my head with a small smile.

But not all guards are focused on the seer. My eyes are locked on Debra, the woman's words running in my mind; her betrayal. "What did you mean we have to send him away?" The king asks, but I understand what she has done. "She's done talking." I sigh, "Thank you for your suggestion. You may let her out." I say to the guards.

The guards open letting her walk away, but they do not rest. Instead they surround the new threat, Debra. "Your majesty, I swear I do not know what she speaks of...Topaz." I can only watch as my old friend is surrounded by the guards she once helped create.

"Sir Ruby." She begs for my husband's pardon. "What betrayal does she speak of?" "Your royal highnesses I swear on my life I would never betray you." "You have shown undying loyalty for your queen, our union, me, and this kingdom." He steps closer to her, "But you must understand that that is not enough to turn a blind eye to such vague accusations." Debra's eyes fall on mine once more before they return to her king.

Defeated, she lowers her sword, "Of course." She says, handing over her weapon to the king. As soon as he takes the weapon she is restrained by the guards. "Take her to the dungeons."

The guards lead her through the same doors she emerged from. I stand, my husband to my left, guards to my right, watching as my dear friend is taken to the dungeons as a traitor.

I created Obsidian's path with three versions in mind.
Each a different length.
The Obsidian's Path versions serve to show the way that time can erode detail for the sake of efficiency in its retelling.

I hope that you will join me on this journey.
Thank you
J. E. O. R.

Instagram:
j.e.o.r.creator_

www.ingramcontent.com/pod-product-compliance
Lightning Source LLC
LaVergne TN
LVHW041237150826
845673LV00008B/2407

9798895698129